MARK OLYNYK

STONES

OF TIME

Contents

TRIVIAL PURSUITS

I'll be there

at the speed of light

when you turn on

your device.

a fiber optic

phantom

haunts your screen.

should you read

my status updates

on the affairs

of state

and other

trivial pursuits

I would be gratified.

you know

it's hard to think of anything

to say

other than speed kills.

but I don't know

about that.

SILENCE IS GOLDEN

the world falls silent

off the grid.

I can only hear myself

thinking

about the noise I am missing.

mindless chatter

and chitchat

from heads

without bodies

to back them up.

when I hear words

of substance

I will listen again.

but I prefer the silent

treatment

because

silence is golden.

STRANGE PLACE

I don't trust a universe

where anything

can happen.

a universe

that acts big

for its age

is easy

to get lost in.

when you no longer

feel at home

a universe

is a strange place

to be living.

cut adrift

in outer space

it's time to pray

for a miracle.

to make it

go away.

MARK OLYNYK

WING AND A PRAYER

I am

making it up on the fly

so I can stop

running away

from the obvious

fact that

something

is always there

waiting

to be said

whether it is true

or not

remains to be seen

but a reality check

is pure fantasy

when I soar

on a wing and a prayer

STONES OF TIME

unafraid

of coming down

to earth

MARK OLYNYK

BETTER OFF

I never noticed

that my mind was going.

I should have seen it coming.

but I was too wrapped up

in my own affairs

to care.

I guess I really didn't need it

anyway.

I'm better off

alone

with no-one there.

to remind me

of past regrets

and remorse

for acts

I would take back

if I could.

REALITY

I was subject

to a subjective experience

of reality.

the object of which

was to experience objects.

this is all I know

everything else is abstract.

that I am here

and not there

is not in dispute.

as a prisoner of circumstances

the object never objects

to being an object.

only the subject

does this.

reality is the object

of my affection.

DREAM-TIME

I must be dreaming

to think that dreams

are heaven sent.

when everyone knows

they come from dream-time.

a nice place to visit

but I wouldn't want

to live there

with pagan gods

in a nightmare scenario.

where logic flew

out the door

and there's no turning back.

be rest assured

there is no sense
in asking why

the impossible

STONES OF TIME

is the rule.

where there is no

free will

my feet are glued to the floor

and I never get away.

from the monsters

in dream-time.

but since when do dreams

come true?

MARK OLYNYK

OVER THE MOON

if I was in the mood

my feelings

on feelings would not be mixed.

on the one hand

feeling good

is good

for your mood.

but all that can change

when you are over the moon

with excitement.

mood swings

hit like sudden rain.

and bad news

leaves you feeling out of sorts

in your frustration.

emotions become a liability

if you let them

STONES OF TIME

run wild.

so my feelings

on feelings are muted.

and the question

is moot.

MARK OLYNYK

WANTED MAN

There is nowhere to go

for a wanted man.

wear a disguise

and everyone knows your name.

hide underground

and your reputation grows.

be low key

and get noticed

for a keynote address.

a wanted man

is just a projection

of your desires

held to a gold standard.

becoming a floating

abstraction
not tethered to reality.

a creature of fantasy

STONES OF TIME

is a construct

only in your

mind.

zigging and zagging.

MARK OLYNYK

SLEIGHT OF HAND

a poet

uses sleight of hand

to pen realities

that are really illusions.

like a magician

conjuring

new ideas

out of thin air.

that are old before their time.

since there is nothing new

under the sun.

making something

out of nothing

is a good parlour trick.

saying one thing

but meaning something else.

is another way

of saying

nothing at all.

DARK TIMES

This much is certain.

the only truth

is uncertainty.

and where does this leave me?

being kept in the dark

would be better

than this.

knowing that I know nothing

for sure

tells me nothing

I need to know.

since I don't really

believe it

in the first place.

COMMON MAN

the answer

in a blade of grass

that whispers in a meadow

was a commonplace.

and I never questioned

the source

of its wisdom

that seemed beyond my grasp.

but then

I was reminded

that we are one

with nature.

and what is more common

than that?

SOLE OWNER

You are the sole owner

of a soul.

souls can be filled

with holes.

some holes

are really souls.

a hole is not whole

unless it is filled.

it will take some

soul searching

to consider

the solitary confinement

of the soul

as a good thing.

after all

the soul is the sole occupant

of my body.

TOWER

the tower of Babel

towers over history

in a babble

of voices

that are never tongue tied.

in a game

where everyone

is at your throat.

everything is tongue

in cheek.

when they threaten

to disarm you

with tongue twisters

hard to unravel

at the best of times.

it is clear

from the rabble

they believe

the tower will never fall.

as long as they

stay on

speaking terms.

BODY LANGUAGE

a body is the last to know

something is up.

when the whole world

is against him

a body must be wide awake

to the threat

and watch his back.

if he turns too fast

he will fall.

and body armour

will not protect him

from the slings and arrows

that a body of evidence

will produce.

if he dares

to assert his right

to happiness

and stand up

straight.

body language

never lies.

MIDDLEMAN

if you are feeling

squeezed in the middle

and getting it

from both sides.

a middleman may be

of service

to negotiate a truce.

between our better angels

and the fallen ones

who bedevil us

with their charms.

in a moral conflict

as old as man.

his position

is always

middle of the road.

and the cost

is not cheap.

but this will have to do.

SOCIAL LADDER

know your place

in polite society.

it is rude

to rock the boat

with so many people

dependent

on the system.

any suggestion

of a deviation

from accepted cultural norms

is frowned upon.

you must start

at the bottom

and climb your way

to the top

of the social ladder.

or no one will give you

the time of day.

with proper credentials

you might get a chance

to make

a contribution.

as long as nothing

is changed.

ROBOT BONES

WHEN the sun has set

at last

on mankind

what will remain

for alien

archaeologists

to learn

when they sift

through the sands

of time

and robot bones

in subterranean cities

are the only

trace

left behind?

HISTORY

History is behind

the times.

it never seems

to catch up with today

which is always one step ahead

of yesterday.

and yesterday underlies

everything we do.

like an undercurrent

that tries to alter

the course

of current events.

in a continuation

of the past.

but the influence
of yesterday

is history.

DESTINY

Destiny is the one place

you can get to

by taking

a wrong turn.

No matter which road

you took

it had to be this way.

There is no escape

from destiny.

Destiny is the destination.

We are predestined

to know

our destiny.

The problem is how

to get there.

It is most peculiar

that all roads

end up

here.

BLINDERS

Take the blinders off.

They are binding

your position.

It is only

blind chance

that we ever got this far.

This really puts me

in a bind.

Should I be worried

or relieved?

The law is a binding

proposition.

When I remove

my blindfold

the light is blinding me

to the truth.

And I can only see

the darkness

of my blind spot.

CODE RED

I do not want

to be remembered as a line of code.

I was much more than that

before I was reduced

to an algorithm.

although this may be

a mathematically sound

proposition

it is the equivalent

of a spiritual

Purgatory.

LIMBO

everything came to an end

a long time ago.

we just don't know

we are in limbo.

not really going

anywhere.

whether you believe it

or not

is neither here

nor there.

it's now or never

for now.

it seems all we ever had

was time on our hands

to waste away

after all.

HARVEST TIME

writing leaves me

with blood

on my hands.

when I prune

the branches

that want to veer off

in all directions.

and pull the weeds

that are choking

the growth

of my ideas.

in the field

of imagination

they take root

or whither

on the vine.

and only the hardiest

will survive.

when I separate

the wheat

from the chaff

at harvest

time.

HUMAN BEING

Once I was human

but somewhere

along the line

I lost my humanity.

then everything changed

and not

for the better.

now I'm something else

like a lower order

of animal

maybe.

indifferent

to making a difference.

PUPPETS

We are puppets on a string

tied to the master hand

of fate.

dancing on the stage

of our days

to the rhythm

of the drum.

directed from the wings

on what to say

and do.

who knew

we had no control

over the scenes

we play.

RULING ELITE

we would be little gods

and decide the fate

of worlds

we made on a dare.

given half the chance

we might be rulers

who have

a certain flair

for rolling the dice.

but when it comes

down to it

we are more than qualified.

ALL IN ALL

there is the all

in one

and the one

in all

and

there is the all

for one

but the one is for itself

as if all else

was an afterthought.

ME OR HIM

the ego and the id.

one is seen

one is hid.

ONE IS THE SHIP

ONE IS THE SEA.

one is the way out

one is the way in.

ONE IS ME

ONE IS HIM.

one is the ego

one is the id.

HUNGER GAMES

Eat your hunger

And never go hungry.

Be satisfied

There was no need

To fill.

Is it enough to be free

Of desire?

If you agree

Here lies contentment.

LISTEN UP

Listen to the silence

and it will tell you things

about yourself

only you

need to hear.

But first block out

the background

noise

that traps your ears.

And find yourself

sound

to listen to the years.

LIGHTS OUT

The lights are going out

One by one

And I can't find the switch

To turn them back on.

It used to be on the wall

Of this room

But the room is gone.

Leaving me to conclude:

There never was

A room.

There never was

A light.

REFLECT ON THIS

what is found

on the

inside

is really

only outside

turned inside out.

which makes

the inside

a mirror

image

of the outside.

and we

are

but a reflection.

FORMLESS

the beauty was in the life

not the shape.

the beauty inside

was ideal.

there can be idea

without form.

there can be life

without body.

a place where beauty

was born.

MIND OVER MATTER

real life is only a dream

of real life

in the mind

of all

minds.

but even this is not

what it seems.

after all

what is real

about a dream?

IT SEEMS...

a poet is a sleepwalker

in a daydream.

this makes him absent

minded

and distant.

when you ask him for the time

he might just give it

to you.

and then

where would you be?

if not inside

HIS

dream.

SHADOW PLAY

The sun

Does not cast a shadow.

There is no darkness

In the light.

How can this be?

When the light is understanding

There is nothing to hide.

Not even the shadow play

Of Shades

In the underworld.

APPLE TREE

(IT SEEMS)

there is nothing more to say

for now.

(IF)

I think of something

I'll let you know.

(BECAUSE)

ideas don't grow

on trees.

(UNLESS)

you know where to find

a tree

of knowledge.

LIFE LESSON

life is a miracle

of science

but life

is not supernatural.

because the supernatural

is not natural

there can be no life

outside

of nature.

but there can be a lifeless

SCIENCE.

SINE LANGUAGE

life is like a sine wave.

equal parts

up

and equal parts down.

an oscillation

of moods

in a bi-polar personality.

where hope and despair

co-exist

in an uneasy truce.

never knowing if the way up

is on

the downswing.

THOUGHT FULL

I had a thought

concerning the nature of thoughts.

All thoughts

are just variations

of the one

master thought.

Like a school of fish

in the ocean.

That resist being caught.

It takes

a patient fisherman

to know when to cast his line.

I THINK THAT

A thinker finds it hard to stop

his Thought

in its tracks.

AND

take the time to meditate.

IT SEEMS

he just doesn't have the mindset for it.

BECAUSE

it's hard to train

his Mind

to go against the grain

AND

grind to a screeching

halt.

FLOATER

Sometimes I feel self-contained

And have no trouble

Holding myself together.

At other times

There doesn't seem to be

Enough room

In my body.

Because I get too full

Of myself

I begin to float away.

Unsure whether freedom

Is any better.

SUN DAY

Sun light

lightens my mood

so that I begin to feel light.

like having a spring

in my step

when winter is weighing

me down.

like floating on air

without a worry

or care.

like being buoyed

by hope

when the sea

would rather see me

drown.

LITTLE CONSEQUENCE

a micro-poet thinks

big

in a small

way.

everything seems

small

in

outer space.

and the big

issues

are

of little

consequence.

when you are

accused

of

navel gazing.

look no further

than

the stars

for inspiration.

they know

that

the least is the most

important.

IDENTITY CRISIS

I am

the mountain

I see

the mountain

is me

in an absolute sense

this makes

no sense

why the mountain?

why me?

MARK OLYNYK

FACE TIME

the mountain

intrudes

upon my eyes.

its sheer face

puts me

in my place.

a curtain of rock

blocks out

the sky.

and l am

left

with tunnel vision.

BIRD OF PREY

time flies by

like a bird

of prey

hunting down

our

mortality.

in the dead

of night

there is no sleep

in the grip

of

its talons.

MARK OLYNYK

TWO FOR ONE

The DICHOTOMY

of the soul

gets me down.

when I have to keep

on rolling

that boulder up the hill.

it seems to me

that it is good to reach the top

and bad to hit rock

bottom.

but it's true

that it's good to be in a bad way

to get the push

you need

for UNITY.

TRIED AND TRUE

Experience is the

litmus test

of truth.

And truth

is sometimes

base.

Experience is gained

in fits and starts.

Until it starts

rolling

down

the hill.

Experience is an asset

to be saved

in the memory

bank.

But don't bank

on it.

DESERTED

there will come a time

when the riverbed

is dry

and words

no longer flow

when desert winds blow

the dust of years

into eyes

that find it hard to see

clearly.

in a wasteland

of tears

rolling down a face

of lines.

etched by words

no longer

there.

THE REAL DEAL

We perceive

through

the prism of the senses

a

world

that is conditioned

by

our perception.

But appearances

may be

deceiving

while

reality is TRUE.

ENTROPY

Disintegration

is a part

of the natural order

that leaves

me

troubled

as I try to come to grips

with the

NEED to feed

destruction.

OUT OF REACH

Transcendentalism

IS

quite a reach.

if your objective

is a state

of collective

consciousness

rather than

the run

of the mill variety.

SPACE MAN

the next

time

you're just staring

into space

remember

there is a time

for

everything

and a space

to do

it

in

if

you can

just

get oriented

in time

and

space.

MONKEY BUSINESS

evolution

is the intelligent design

of a revolutionary

planner

looking forward

to the next generation

mass extinction

to

start

over

again…

MARK OLYNYK

MOUSE TRAP

a moral imperative

made me do it.

this is not the same

as free will

because

freedom is free.

from the trappings

of tradition.

ANGRY BIRDS

it is a kind of madness

to get mad.

if you are out of temper

you will

lose your temper.

when you question

the motives

of the questioner.

that leave

your peace of mind

in pieces.

REAPER

the grim reaper

is

grinning

from ear to ear.

he is the only one

who knows

the

end is near.

but it is clear

he is from

far

below.

SURVIVE ALL

many

are the lessons

to be learned

from the

vivisection of

the

undead.

a caricature of truth

would be

one.

as I try

to revive morbidity

that

has gone rigid.

at the

REVIVAL.

VAMP

revamp the vampire.

the genre

has

lost its bite.

rouse the dead

for

old times' sake.

they only come out

at

night.

the hunter

is prey

to passing fancies.

the zombie apocalypse

is a

no-brainer

at the wake.

VIRAL

the plague ignored

the

gag order.

and opened its mouth.

to swallow a ghost

town

hiding

in quarantine.

as the worm turns.

the mouth gets bigger.

and the world

has no

appetite.

for a

starving house

guest.

DISTURBANCE

beware

be

aware.

tranquility traps catching

wisps of

air.

drifting

through crevasses

far

and near.

unseen by human

eyes.

a

breath of fear.

disturbing the

peace

of mind.

WORLDS AWAY

the weight of the world

is hard

to carry around.

tied to my neck

is the

mill stone

of my cares.

in the whole wide

world

there is nowhere

to go.

waiting to catch

a lift.

to put my burden down.

THE END OF TIME

when the universe

ends

I don't want

to be

a part of it.

I will hedge my bets

and wait

for another

one

to unfold.

some say the universe

will stop

when it runs

out

of room.

if that is the case

I want to book

a flight

with another

airline.

and hold out hope

that this

plane

won't crash

and burn.

About The Author

Mark Olynyk is a poet with a philosophical bent. His first published poem was "Null Space" in 1996. This event set off a chain reaction of poetry that continues to this day. His poems have appeared in anthologies and literary journals, such as: The Prairie Journal (2001-2002), Canadian Writer's Journal (2002), Eunoia Review (2013), Poetry Movement Volume II (2016) and Lockdown Poetry (2020). Mark has self-published several poetry books. He can be found on Facebook and X.